Fairytale Princess

Check out Princess Poppy's website
to find out all about the other
books in the series
www.princesspoppy.com

Princess Poppy Fairytale Princess

written by Janey Louise Jones
Illustrated by Samantha Chaffey

FAIRYTALE PRINCESS
A YOUNG CORGI BOOK 978 0 552 55921 8

Published in Great Britain by Young Corgi,
an imprint of Random House Children's Books
A Random House Group Company

This edition published 2009

1 3 5 7 9 10 8 6 4 2

Young Corgi Books are published by Random House Children's Books,
61–63 Uxbridge Road, London W5 5SA

www.princesspoppy.com
www.rbooks.co.uk

Addresses for companies within The Random House Group Limited can be found at: www.randomhouse.co.uk/offices.htm

THE RANDOM HOUSE GROUP Limited Reg. No. 954009

A CIP catalogue record for this book is available from the British Library.

Printed and bound in Germany

Especially for Amelie Primrose,

a little fairy princess

Honeypot Hill

To the City
Saffron Thimble's Sewing shop
The Orchards
Paddle Steamer Quay
Healing House & Garden
The Worthington's House
Lavender Valley Garden Centre
Aunt
Melody Maker's Music shop
Lavender Lake
Bumble Bee's Teashop
Lavender Lake School of Dance
Hedgerows Hotel (where Mimosa lives)
SCHOOL
Peppermint Pond
Rosehip School
Summer Meadow
Christmas Corner
Wildspice Woods

oneysuckle Cottage
(Poppy's House)

N
W
E
S

Poppy Field

Forget-Me-Not Cottage
Grandpa's House + office

t Cottage
anny

Blossom
Bakehouse

Cornsilk Castle
and
Courtyard

golds
re

Village Hall

Sage's Vet Surgery

t Office

Beehive
Beauty Salon

Riverside
stables

Barley Farm
The Meadowsweet's
House

River Swan

Honeypot Hill
Railway Station

To Camomile Cove
via Periwinkle Lane

Chapter One

Poppy thought that her teacher, Miss Mallow, was absolutely brilliant. She was so kind and she was always thinking up ways to make her lessons really interesting and fun. Poppy especially loved Monday mornings because every week they had what Miss Mallow called "circle time". This was when each and every one of the children was given an opportunity to share something that was special to them with the rest of the class. It was called "circle time" because Miss Mallow made them put their chairs in a big circle in the middle of the classroom so that they could all see everything that was being shown.

Poppy nearly always brought in something.

One Monday, she was especially pleased with what she had brought – it was one of her most treasured possessions and she couldn't wait to show it. When Miss Mallow announced that it was circle time, everyone moved their chairs into position and then she went round the class asking each child if they had anything to share. By the time she came to Poppy, Poppy was almost bursting with excitement! She reached into her school bag, pulled out her special item and held it up for everyone to see.

"I got this from my grandpa. It's a book of fairytales and Grandpa told me that it is over a hundred years old! It belonged to Grandpa's granny, who was my great-great-granny Mellow!"

"That is lovely!" exclaimed Miss Mallow. " A true piece of history. In fact, it might be useful today. You see, I have something to share with all of you too."

CINDERELLA

"Maybe she's getting married to Prince Charming!" whispered Poppy to her best friend, Honey. But that was not Miss Mallow's news.

"Children, as you know, builders are working on the school hall at the moment and it is due to be ready in eight weeks," began Miss Mallow. "The stage will be redesigned with new lighting and scenery, there will be new flooring, the roof is being fixed so there will be no more leaks, and we'll have some lovely new chairs and curtains. The Headmistress has invited a special guest to reopen the hall. However, I think we should do something to make the reopening even more special so I've decided that we will put on our very own musical show! What do you think?"

"Yeah!" chorused the whole class.

"Yes, Poppy, what is it?" asked Miss Mallow, noticing that Poppy's hand had gone up as soon as she'd told everyone about her plan.

"Um, who is the special guest? And which show are we going to do?"

"Well, I was actually just coming to both things," smiled Miss Mallow, thinking how impatient and inquisitive Poppy was. "The guest is Bryony Snow, editor of top fashion magazine – Buttons and Bows. We need to impress Ms Snow – if she likes the show she is going to do a feature on it in the magazine, but most importantly we must put on a fabulous event for everyone in the village who has helped us to raise so much money for the hall."

All the girls in the class interrupted Miss Mallow with a huge cheer – Buttons and Bows was their favourite magazine, even though it was for grown-ups.

"But what is the show?" called out Tom impatiently.

"Well," continued Miss Mallow, "I'm going

to write it myself but the words and songs will be based on a well-known story. You all know lots of stories so I thought it might be fun if you helped me to choose. You tell me your ideas and I'll write them on the board. Poppy's lovely storybook might give you some inspiration."

Every single child started calling out their favourites before Miss Mallow had even finished speaking – she could hardly keep up with them!

"Snow White and the Seven Dwarfs," called out one girl.

"Annie!" yelled another.

"Sleeping Beauty," suggested Lola, peering over to look in Poppy's book.

"Treasure Island!" shouted Charlie, to a loud cheer from the other boys.

"Little Red Riding Hood," said Helena.

"Cinderella!" cried Poppy, looking wistfully at the exquisite pictures in Great-Great-Granny Mellow's fairytale book.

"Yeah, Cinderella!" agreed several other girls. "We love Cinderella."

"Peter Pan!" yelled Ollie.

Snow White & the Seven Dwarfs
Annie
Sleeping Beauty
Treasure Island
Little Red Riding Hood
Cinderella
Peter Pan

"Enough!" gasped Miss Mallow. "My wrist is quite numb. We've got plenty to choose from now. I suggest you all copy down this list and have a good think about it overnight. Then tomorrow we can put it to a vote. The story with the most votes is the show that we will do."

At break, Poppy, Honey, Sweetpea, Mimosa and Abi formed a huddle in the playground – they were desperate to talk about the show.

"Which story are you going to vote for?" asked Poppy.

"Cinderella!" replied the other four girls in unison – each imagining themselves in a starring role and dressed as a fairytale princess.

Chapter Two

The next morning there was a buzz of excitement among the children because it was time to vote for their favourite show. The previous evening Miss Mallow had cut up pieces of paper for them to use as voting slips. As she handed one out to each child, she explained how the voting process worked.

"Write down the name of one story only, your favourite, then fold your voting slip very neatly in half and place it in the box on my desk. There's no need to write your name on the slip. Voting should always be secret. Does everyone understand?" she asked.

"Yes, miss!" chorused the class.

Before long everyone had placed their folded slip in the shoebox. Miss Mallow cleared the top of her desk and started to unfold the pieces of paper in order to count the votes, but when she looked at them, her face fell.

"Oh, dear! Some of you have written down more than one story. That's not the idea at all. It has to be just your favourite. I can't count these as proper votes."

A few people blushed. They hadn't been listening when Miss Mallow was explaining what to do. Poppy and Honey were annoyed as they were impatient to know which story would win – it was always the same few people who didn't listen and spoiled things.

Miss Mallow asked everyone to stop chatting. "We'll have to do it all over again!" she sighed. "Luckily I made extra voting slips. Now, everyone, look at the board and I will tell you once more what to do."

Finally they all managed to cast their votes successfully.

"I'll lock these votes in my desk drawer for now and take them out after break," said Miss Mallow. "At the beginning of our next lesson I'll count them in front of you. Then we'll have a result and I can be writing the show in time for you to start rehearsals. Now go out and play!"

Poppy and her friends couldn't concentrate on their usual break-time activities like hopscotch or cat's cradle – they were desperate to know what the show would be. They all just sat on the wall with their milk and biscuits,

wishing break would end so they could hear the results.

When they went back into class and settled at their desks, Miss Mallow greeted them with one of her warm smiles.

"Please take out your *Reading for Fun* books and read quietly while I count the votes," she said as she started to sort the slips into separate piles – one for each show.

When she had done this, she counted the number of slips in each pile, eagerly watched by the whole class – none of them could concentrate on the reading task she had set them.

At last Miss Mallow looked up.

"Put down your books – we have a result!"

Everyone was dying to hear but they were so excited they were being very noisy.

"I won't announce anything until you settle down!" said their teacher.

Everyone fell silent immediately.

"The shows with the most votes," began Miss Mallow, "are Treasure Island and Cinderella."

Some children cheered and others booed, disappointed that their favourite was not in the top two. Again Miss Mallow had to ask everyone to calm down.

"It is extremely close: there is only one vote between these two!" she told them. "And the winner is . . . Cinderella!"

There was lots of cheering and whooping, but also some booing, mainly from the boys, as they thought Cinderella was too girlie to be any fun.

"Miss Mallow," said Charlie, putting up his hand, "Harvey is ill today and he told me he was definitely going to vote for Treasure Island, so that would have been a draw!"

Before Miss Mallow could reply, Mimosa piped up. "Miss," she said, "Lola is ill today too,

and she was going to vote for Cinderella, I know she was, so it would still have won!"

"Class, settle down immediately!" said Miss Mallow firmly. "We simply will not be able to carry on with this if you won't accept the result of the vote. I'm in charge and I cannot take into account people who are not here. Cinderella has won fair and square so that is the show we'll be doing. I won't hear another word about it. Please take out your rough jotters and put the date in the margin and write a heading: Sentences."

Everyone usually groaned when Miss Mallow said this, but this time they did as she said, in silence. They could tell that she was annoyed and they didn't want to be properly told off. Miss Mallow was the best teacher in the world and hardly ever got cross, but when she did, it was very serious indeed.

Miss Mallow spent her whole lunch hour noting down ideas for the show. She was very excited about it – she had never done anything like this before. She really hoped that the children would have fun and that the Headmistress, Mrs Milkthistle – as well as the school governors – would be impressed with it.

Towards the end of the day, Miss Mallow spoke to the class about the show.

"Please listen carefully," she began. "Now that we have chosen our show, we need to start rehearsing. The first rehearsal will be a week on Friday, straight after school, and it will take the form of auditions for each part."

"What are auditions?" asked Tom.

"It's when you act out a little bit of one character's lines to see if you are good at being that character," explained Miss Mallow. "I will give you a script and a character list before that so you can decide which parts to try out for. Remember, if you'd rather help backstage or play an instrument in the orchestra, that's a very important part of any show. Not everybody likes acting. Now, please take these permission letters home to your parents and bring back the signed reply slips before next Friday. We will be rehearsing every Friday for six weeks, and on the seventh week we'll do our performance of the show."

When Poppy saw Mum at the school gates, she ran towards her and handed her the permission letter.

"And the auditions are next Friday, Mum!" she told her. "I really, really hope I'm Cinderella.

She's my favourite ever fairytale princess!"

"Well, Poppy, you're certainly a natural actress! But we'll just have to wait and see," said Mum.

Poppy lay in bed that night gazing at her great-great-granny's book of fairytales and fell asleep dreaming of a fairy godmother waving a wand and giving her the role of Cinderella.

Chapter Three

The next day Miss Mallow told her class all about the history of the story of Cinderella. This was one of the reasons why Poppy thought she was such a brilliant teacher. Poppy loved knowing lots of little details – they made things that might have been boring seem really interesting.

"Did you know," began Miss Mallow, "that there are versions of this story from every corner of the world, all dating back hundreds of years? But the most popular version was written by Charles Perrault in 1697. He added more details to the traditional folktale – like the pumpkin, the Fairy Godmother and the glass slippers. In fact, at first he thought of fur slippers, but then he realized they would be too stretchy! Can anyone tell the class the story as we know it nowadays?"

Poppy's hand shot straight up in the air. She knew this tale inside out and back to front. She had so often imagined how sad Cinderella must have felt at the start of the story and how happy at the end.

"OK then, Princess Poppy!" smiled Miss Mallow. "Come out to the front and tell us the story of Cinderella!"

Poppy stood behind Miss Mallow's desk, cleared her throat and began to tell the

story. When she had finished, everyone clapped, amazed at how well Poppy knew it.

That week the children could think of nothing but the school show – even the boys were becoming quite enthusiastic about being on stage. Everyone was dying to see the new hall, which was strictly out of bounds while the builders were there. No one was allowed in until the week before the show, so the rehearsals were going to take place in the gym instead.

At the start of the following week, Miss Mallow handed a script and cast list to each child in her class.

"Here we have the script for the Rosehip School musical version of Cinderella, and a cast list for auditions too. Please study these before Friday and come to the rehearsal with an idea of which parts you would like to try out for," she said.

The whole class pored over the list.

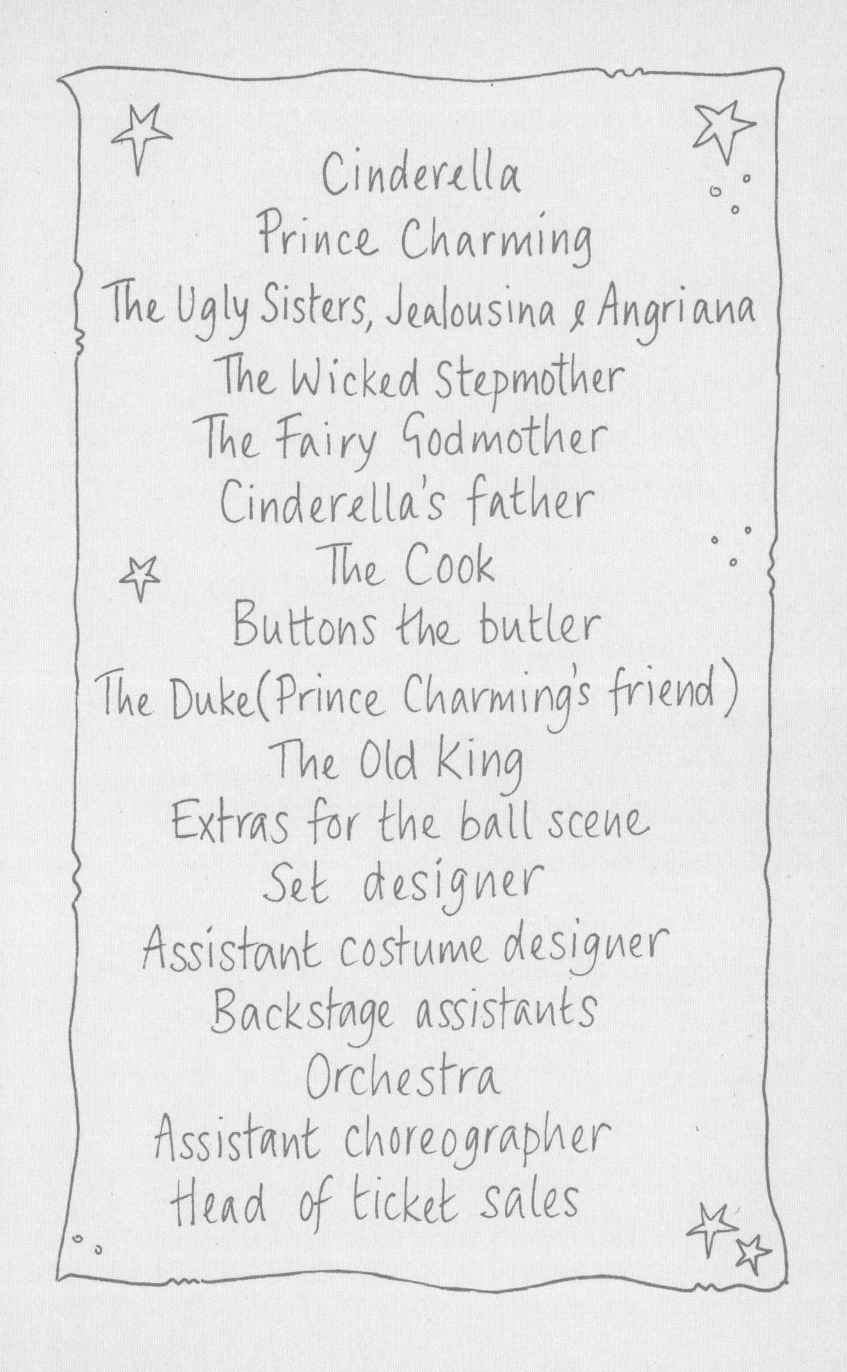
Cinderella
Prince Charming
The Ugly Sisters, Jealousina & Angriana
The Wicked Stepmother
The Fairy Godmother
Cinderella's father
The Cook
Buttons the butler
The Duke (Prince Charming's friend)
The Old King
Extras for the ball scene
Set designer
Assistant costume designer
Backstage assistants
Orchestra
Assistant choreographer
Head of ticket sales

"Oh, I hope I'm picked to be Cinderella!" said Poppy. "There aren't really any other parts I like!"

"Me too," said Sweetpea.

"And me!" said Mimosa and Abigail at the same time.

"Well, I hope I'm the Fairy Godmother," said Honey, who loved fairies above all else.

When the end of the week arrived and everyone had finally brought in their permission slips, Miss Mallow's class stayed behind after school. They had a snack in the classroom and then made their way to the gym. Lots of the parents had offered to help with the show – much to Miss Mallow's delight, as she was beginning to realize that it was going to involve a huge amount of work and there was no way she could do it alone. Mr Melody, Abi's dad, had offered to be the musical director. Poppy's cousin Saffron, who was also Miss Mallow's best friend, promised that she would help with the costumes and Poppy's mum had volunteered to make any hats or headpieces. Madame Angelwing, Poppy's ballet teacher, was very kindly going to lend a hand with the dance routines. It was going to be a real team effort.

The children sat in a circle as Miss Mallow explained how the auditions would work. She wrote the names of each character on a card and told everyone who wanted to try out for that part to line up behind the card, but when she looked up, she saw that every single girl

– except Honey – was standing behind the Cinderella card and every single boy was behind the Prince Charming one. She smiled.

"Oh, dear! I thought this might happen!" she said. "You do realize that we can only have one Cinderella and one Prince, don't you? There are lots of other brilliant parts. Playing baddies and meanies like the Ugly Sisters and the Wicked Stepmother is often even more fun than playing princes and princesses. Those are the parts that everyone in the audience will really enjoy!"

But the children weren't convinced and no one would audition for the parts of the Ugly Sisters or the Wicked Stepmother.

"Come on, class!" said Miss Mallow. "It's too late to choose another show – and may I remind you that a majority of you did vote for Cinderella. You can't all have thought you'd be Cinderella or Prince Charming!"

But she saw from the look on their faces that it was exactly what they had thought!

"Please will you have another think about it – otherwise we're not going to get anywhere," said Miss Mallow, despair creeping into her voice. "There are lots of other parts, plus all the important non-acting roles. Come on, children. You've got five minutes."

Some of the boys moved around a bit and one, Tom Worthington, volunteered to be Cinderella's father. Honey had already said that she would like to play the Fairy Godmother. Gradually other children began to move around and stand behind different cards. For most of the parts there was no need for an audition as only one child had put themselves forward. But for the parts of Cinderella and Prince Charming there was still a great deal of competition. Poppy and several other girls, all of whom wanted to be the star of the show, weren't budging. There was no way they were going to give up the opportunity of being their all-time favourite fairytale princess that easily.

The girls formed a queue for trying out as Cinderella, each doing her absolute best when her moment came. Poppy was second last in the line, with just Abi behind her. As each of her friends made a brilliant job of their audition, she became more and more nervous. By the time it was her go, she was sick with nerves.

Ever since Miss Mallow had given out the scripts, Poppy had been trying to memorize the part of Cinderella. But now she was so nervous that she decided to use the script again – just in case.

"Come on then, Poppy," said Miss Mallow.

"It's your turn now."

She walked to the front of the gym, trying hard to imagine how sad and lonely Cinderella must have felt without a kind mother like hers – and how tired after all the housework the stepsisters made her do. She only had to look at her script once during the whole audition and was quite pleased with how it had gone.

"Well done!" said Honey when Poppy had finished. "You were really good."

All the girls, including Poppy, had done really well in their auditions for the part of Cinderella. Poor Miss Mallow had a tough decision to make. She scratched her head and looked back at the

notes she had made about each performance. She liked Poppy's energy and spirit, but she liked Abi's singing voice – and it was lovely to see a shy girl blossom through drama. Lola had a beautifully clear speaking voice and Sweetpea had put so much feeling into her performance. All the other girls had been great in their own ways and all of them would make lovely Cinderellas.

Oh, dear. What am I going to do? thought Miss Mallow.

However, she didn't have time to dwell on it – she had to get on and cast the rest of the play. But by the end of the session she still had no Ugly Sisters or a Wicked Stepmother.

When it was time to go home, Miss Mallow told her class that she would spend the weekend thinking about who was best for each role and would announce the cast on Monday. Poppy sighed – she couldn't bear the prospect of spending another weekend without knowing if she was going to be Cinderella or not.

What if Miss Mallow didn't choose her – who would she be? Poppy shuddered at the very thought of being made to play one of the Ugly Sisters!

Chapter Four

Miss Mallow spent a long time thinking about the auditions and who she should choose for the main parts. She re-read the script, only to realize how few good parts there actually were in the story, especially considering the size of her class. Then she had an idea!

Hmmm, I suppose I am the writer of this show, so I could create a few new characters, she thought.

Miss Mallow decided to write in a sister for Prince Charming and named her Princess Ursula, and a cousin for Buttons called Rose. Then she added a Hunter and a Horseman to the Prince's staff. But even when she'd finished, she still wasn't sure who would play which part. She hoped that if there were some new characters, the children would not be too disappointed if they were not Cinderella or Prince Charming.

"But I still want to make the choosing as fair as possible," she said to herself.

On Sunday Miss Mallow had arranged to meet Saffron at the Lavender Lake School of Dance. Madame Angelwing had invited them both over to see whether there was anything in the costume room that they might like to use for the show.

"Thank you so much for letting us look around, Madame Angelwing," said Miss Mallow as she took in all the gorgeous costumes and accessories.

"It is a pleasure, Miss Mallow. Just make sure you note down anything you borrow in the costume book," Madame Angelwing replied as she glided off to her office.

Just then Miss Mallow noticed a rack of shoes and had a spark of inspiration – she couldn't wait to share it with her class!

"Good morning, everyone!" she said to them on Monday morning. "I've been thinking about the play and I've had some ideas that I think you'll like. In some cases I've decided who will play which parts, but I've also written in some exciting new characters. However, for the roles of Prince Charming and Cinderella I have a further little test because you were all so good it was impossible to choose between you."

The children were desperate to hear her ideas, especially what the extra test would be.

"I will reveal everything in a minute. In the meantime, here is a list of the parts already decided," said Miss Mallow as she flipped the board over. "If your name isn't on it, you are being considered for the roles of Prince Charming or Cinderella and will have to take the additional test."

CINDERELLA .... to be confirmed
PRINCE CHARMING .... to be confirmed
THE UGLY SISTERS .... to be confirmed
THE WICKED STEPMOTHER..... to be confirmed
THE FAIRY GODMOTHER ..... Honey Bumble
CINDERELLA'S FATHER .... Tom Worthington
THE COOK .... to be confirmed
BUTTONS .... to be confirmed
BUTTON'S COUSIN, ROSE .... to be confirmed
THE DUKE .... to be confirmed
THE OLD KING .... Archie Simmons
PRINCESS URSULA ..... to be confirmed
THE HUNTER .... to be confirmed
THE HORSEMAN .... to be confirmed
EXTRAS FOR THE BALL SCENE ... Martha, ... Fifi, Helena and Lara
SET DESIGNER .... Lara
ASSISTANT COSTUME DESIGNER .... Rachel
ORCHESTRA ... Angus, Hamish, Harvey, Sarah and Jane.
ASSISTANT CHOREOGRAPHER ..... Martha
HEAD OF TICKET SALES ...... Jasmine

"You'll notice that there are still a lot of parts left to cast and we'll get to that. But first, let me tell you about the main roles. A lot of you wanted to be Prince Charming and Cinderella but there can only be one of each, so I've come up with something to help me choose. I have here a pair of very dainty 'glass slippers'. Actually, they are just very sparkly silver ones from the Lavender Lake School of Dance costume room! I've also got a pair of black patent Prince Charming shoes. These are the shoes that we will use in the show, so whoever they fit the best will be Cinderella and the Prince. And the rest of you will take the remaining parts without complaining. Does that sound fair?"

Everyone nodded but Poppy was really worried – what if they didn't fit?

Miss Mallow put the sparkly slippers on her desk and the girls queued up to try them on. Sweetpea went first. No luck – they were far too small. She looked very sad. Mimosa tried, and Lola too. Again, they did not fit – they were simply too narrow. When it was Poppy's turn she tried to force her foot into the pretty shoe. It was a terrible squeeze – her heel simply wouldn't go in, however hard she tried. She sighed – like the others, her feet were just not dainty enough for the exquisite antique shoes. The last person to try on the slippers was Abi. While her feet weren't particularly small, they were unusually narrow. As she slid her foot into the

silver slipper, all the other girls gasped. It was a perfect fit!

"Well, these do fit well!" smiled Miss Mallow. "I was beginning to think they wouldn't fit anyone. It looks like we have our Cinderella!"

Abi beamed with delight. She had never been picked for anything like this before. But Poppy and all the other girls were very, very disappointed. A huge black cloud settled over Poppy; she thought she would never be happy again. She tried to be pleased for her friend and was determined not to cry in front of everyone, but deep down she felt very sad – it was all because of her stupid wide feet!

"Girls, please don't be upset. There are other fun parts and lots of chances to wear pretty dresses," said Miss Mallow. "But before we sort that out, we need to choose our Prince Charming. Up to the front, boys!"

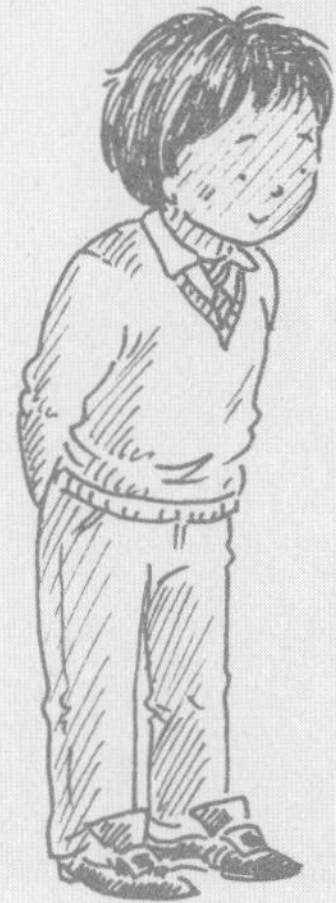

She then tried the Prince's shoes on the boys and Charlie Beaches was chosen for Prince Charming.

"Abi! You'll have to marry Charlie!" shouted out Billy Baxter.

"Abi for Charlie!" called Sweetpea.

Abi blushed.

The boys who had missed out seemed to take it better than the girls and they were just keen to hear who would play the other parts.

"Right," said Miss Mallow, "we have our Cinderella and Prince Charming, so now I can decide who will play the remaining parts. As you can see, there are two new girl parts on the list – Princess Ursula and Rose. Sweetpea, you will be Princess Ursula; Poppy, you will be Rose!"

Sweetpea and Poppy both smiled weakly and accepted the new parts. Both girls were trying very hard to hide their disappointment at missing out on the main starring role.

Lola was given the part of the Cook, which she was secretly quite pleased with as she adored cooking and even had her own chef's hat! Mimosa was told that she would play the Wicked Stepmother. At first she was upset because she didn't want to play such a horrid person, but she loved acting and soon realized that she could make the part really special – plus it was an important role.

"Now, children, who are the funniest people in this class?" asked Miss Mallow. "The ones who make us laugh the most and the ones who make me cross most often?"

"Freddie and Ollie!" everyone said in unison as they turned to look at the terrible Morrison twins.

As usual, they were up to mischief and not paying attention to Miss Mallow!

"Boys," began the teacher, "you know how stories like Cinderella sometimes have boys dressed as girls? Well, I've decided that you two are going to be the Ugly Sisters."

Everyone giggled – they could just picture the twins larking around as Jealousina and Angriana, with hideous outfits and make-up, complete with warts and wigs.

"But Miss Mallow, I don't want to dress up as a girl. That's so sissy!" complained Ollie.

"Me neither," agreed Freddie.

"Aw, go on," cried Charlie. "They're the best parts in the show after Prince Charming – even

if you do have to wear dresses!"

"Yeah, you'd be really funny – to look at!" laughed Tom.

"Go on, boys, you'll be excellent – you're both perfect for these roles," said Miss Mallow encouragingly.

"Oh, OK then," said Ollie, poking his twin in the ribs. "I'll do it, but only if Freddie does."

Freddie nodded. He always agreed with Ollie.

Miss Mallow filled in the remaining gaps in the cast list. Now that this was done, the show could really come together. The children accepted their teacher's decisions, even though most of them were very sad that they weren't in the starring roles.

After the rehearsal, Mum knew by the look on Poppy's face that she had not been given the role of Cinderella.

"There'll be other times, sweetheart, and it will be lovely for Abi."

"But why don't I ever get to be the star?" complained Poppy.

"But you are a star. You don't need to be on stage to shine," said Mum, which cheered Poppy a tiny bit.

Chapter Five

Poppy was bitterly disappointed at first but she gradually got used to the idea that she was not Cinderella; she decided to make a really good job of the part of Rose and get involved in the play as much as possible.

The first proper rehearsal on the following Friday started off well, with Miss Mallow feeling very excited and the children equally so. Poppy looked at her script as they all waited for their teacher to photocopy some extra sets for those children who had forgotten or mislaid theirs. She loved Miss Mallow's retelling of the story – it made her favourite fairytale even better!

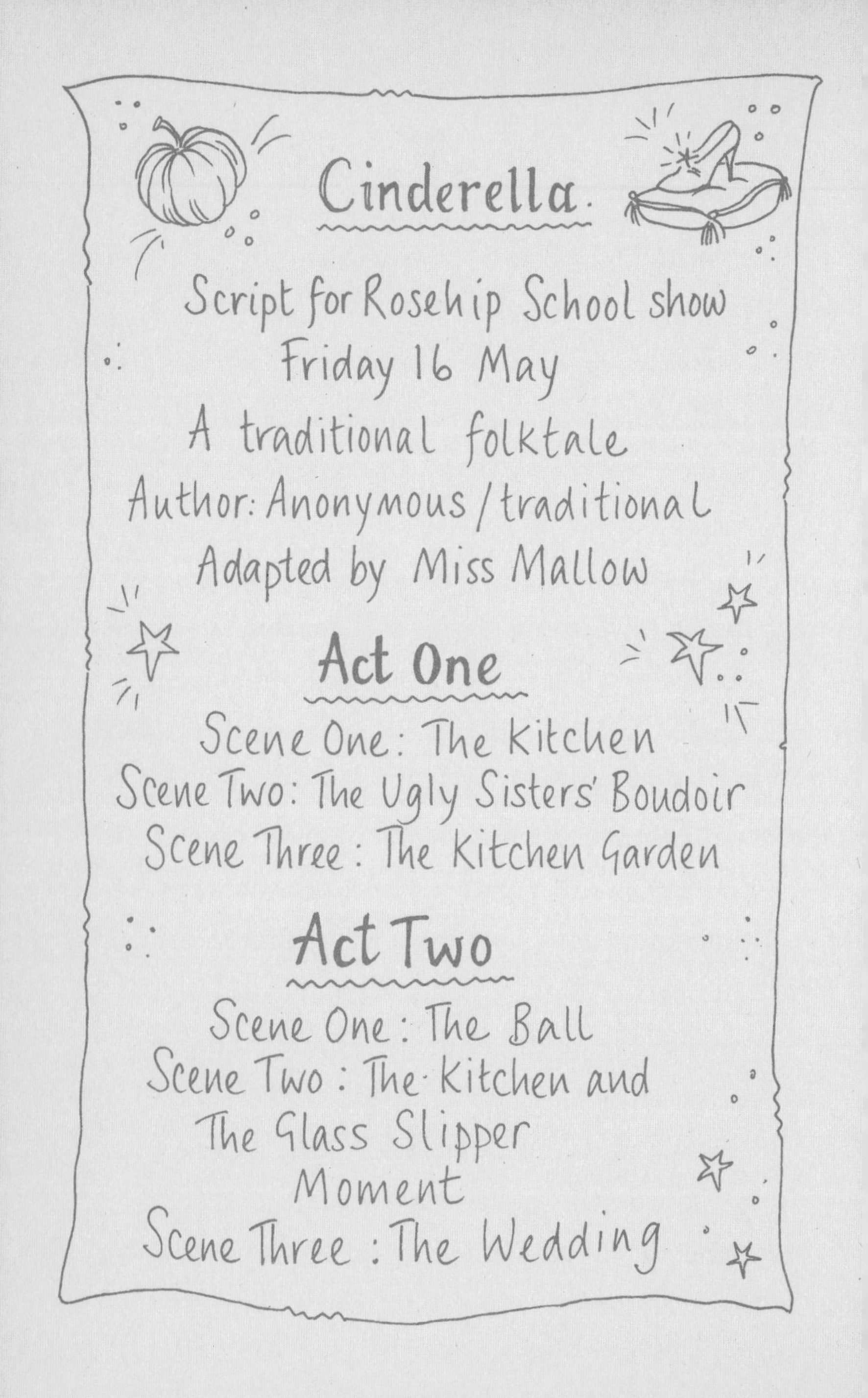

Cinderella
Script for Rosehip School show
Friday 16 May
A traditional folktale
Author: Anonymous / traditional
Adapted by Miss Mallow
Act One
Scene One: The Kitchen
Scene Two: The Ugly Sisters' Boudoir
Scene Three: The Kitchen Garden
Act Two
Scene One: The Ball
Scene Two: The Kitchen and The Glass Slipper Moment
Scene Three: The Wedding

"Before we start running through Act One, Scene One, can I have some volunteers for some of these jobs, please?" said Miss Mallow, pointing to a list on the board.

Poppy offered to design the programmes, while Honey and Sweetpea said they would make the tickets and some of the boys agreed to take posters round all the local shops.

"I will be sitting in the wings to prompt anyone who forgets their lines," explained Miss Mallow. "I think that is almost everything taken care of now. Take your positions on the stage area for the first scene in the kitchen."

But as the children were making their way up, Mimosa piped up: "Please, Miss Mallow, I just want to tell Poppy something about the programme. I think my name should be on the front and in big letters because I am the main character. After all, there would be no story without the Wicked Stepmother and no one else really wanted to be her, so I have done the class a favour."

Before Miss Mallow could say anything, Freddie joined in: "You're not the main part. We are! Everyone knows the Ugly Sisters get the biggest laughs – when Cinderella is on up in the City at Christmas, the Ugly Sisters are always the main characters on the posters."

"No way!" shouted Sweetpea, sticking up for her friend, Abi. "Cinderella is the star. If anyone should have her name in big letters, it's Abigail Melody!"

"Yes, but I wanted to be Cinderella!" exclaimed Lola, who was playing the Cook. "Why should my name be in small letters just because Abi's foot fitted in a little shoe!"

"Yeah!" agreed Billy. "I don't think it was fair using the shoes. It should have been based on how good we were at the auditions, shouldn't it?"

"I was off that day! I could have been Prince Charming!" chimed in Nathan.

And so the squabbling and moaning went on, until Miss Mallow could not stand it any longer.

"Quiet, everyone! I tried my best to be fair –

cat

I explained my reasons for doing the shoe test. I thought you all understood that. Each and every one of you is absolutely vital to this production, however big or small your part, whether you are acting or helping backstage. If anyone were to drop out now, then there would be a problem, wouldn't there? Now, enough of this nonsense! Get on the stage and let's run through the kitchen scene. After that I will tell you about the song and dance moves for this scene. We have a lot to learn and we certainly don't have time to bicker!"

It was very rare for Miss Mallow to lose her temper, and although she hadn't raised her voice, the children knew she was cross. They silently shuffled onto the stage, took their positions and waited for further instructions.

Miss Mallow's special version of the story, with just six simple scenes, was designed to make it easy to move the scenery around without too many complicated changes. It seemed to Poppy that some people did not appreciate all the hard work that their teacher had done and she felt sorry for Miss Mallow. Even though Poppy was still secretly disappointed about not being Cinderella, she wanted the show to be a huge hit – but most of the class didn't seem to care.

When no one knew their lines, even though they had now had the script for almost two weeks, Miss Mallow felt rather worried. The run-through of the first scene was very messy.

"Did anyone read through their lines during the week?" she asked.

Poppy, Abi and Honey raised their hands, but no one else did.

"Well, you had all better come back next Friday with a better attitude and with your lines word perfect – the show will not happen if you don't put the work in! I can't learn your lines for you!" said Miss Mallow, just as the parents arrived to collect their children.

As she tidied everything away after the children had gone, she felt very tired and low. She really wanted to impress Bryony Snow – it would be such a privilege to appear in Buttons and Bows magazine: all her friends read it. But the children were being so difficult and she wasn't sure what she could do to make things better. Perhaps she wasn't up to such a big project after all. Just then she remembered that she was going out for supper at the Hedgerows Hotel with her friend Saffron Sage and Poppy's mum, Lavender Cotton, and she began to feel a bit better. They were meeting to discuss the costumes as Saffron and Lavender had both offered to help. She was sure they would have some good advice for her.

"Are you OK, Holly?" asked Saffron when she saw her friend.

"Oh, I'm fine, thanks. I'm just tired and my class were absolute horrors at the rehearsal this afternoon. But it'll all be worth it in the end," she replied, not sounding terribly convinced by her own words.

"Well, I think you're doing a wonderful job," said Lavender. "I know Poppy is determined to make it the best show ever, plus we're here to help you!"

Holly Mallow smiled. She knew her friends would make her feel better. And when Saffron showed her some truly wonderful sketches for the costumes, she almost forgot how disastrous the rehearsal had been and how upset she was at her class's lack of commitment.

To start off with there was a grey and brown rag dress for Cinderella, which managed to look quite stylish; then, for later, a fabulous pale pink ball gown, followed by the most dreamy white wedding dress imaginable.

"Oh, Saffron, these are gorgeous!" said Miss Mallow.

Then Lavender showed some magazine clippings and sketches of special hats and headpieces for each character.

"Wow! These are amazing! I don't know where you get the time," enthused the teacher.

"I'm so pleased that you like them," said Lavender. "I've had such fun, especially with the Ugly Sisters' hats!"

She and Saffron had reminded their friend what fun it would be to put on the show – and impress Bryony Snow. Miss Mallow was re-inspired. That's what friends were for, after all.

"I've had a great evening!" she said. "I can't wait for the performance now that you have made it come alive – just as long as everybody learns their lines!"

Chapter Six

On Monday Miss Mallow announced that all homework would be based on Cinderella until the show was over. She was sure this would be a good way to keep the children's interest levels up. She wanted them to become familiar with not just their own part, but with every part in the show – as well as the stage directions, the songs, costumes and dances.

"Think of reading through the script as reading homework – and I'll also set you other tasks to do with Cinderella, such as writing a paragraph about your favourite character. The better you understand the whole show, the more we can help make it the best performance ever," she explained.

The class cheered, delighted to get a break from regular homework – they were sure this would be much easier.

In addition to the show-themed homework, Miss Mallow found fun ways of bringing Cinderella into their lessons. One day they had a Cinderella spelling test. Poppy was quite proud of her paper as she normally found spelling really hard.

Poppy Cotton Spelling Test
Wicked
Cinderella
Ugly
Ball
Housework
Pumkin x pumpkin
Coach
Fairy Godmother
Wedding
Slipers x slippers
8/10 Well done, Poppy!

The next day there was a Cinderella maths test.

Rosehip School Maths Test

1. If there are 18 children involved in the school show and 10 are acting on stage, how many are doing non-acting jobs?
2. If the Ugly Sisters had size 10 feet and the glass slippers were size 4, how many sizes too small were they?
3. If Buttons had 12 buttons on his best jacket and 12 on his old jacket, how many buttons were there altogether on the two jackets?
4. If Cinderella did 10 jobs a day for the Ugly Sisters, how many jobs did she do for them in a week?

Most days after school, Poppy, Honey, Abi, Sweetpea and Mimosa went to each other's houses to rehearse their lines. They didn't want Miss Mallow to be disappointed again on Friday. But they ended up chatting about how fantastic the show would be and how spectacular they would all look rather than actually learning their lines.

By mid-week, Poppy and Honey realized that they didn't know their parts as well as they should, so in addition to meeting up with the others to talk about the show, they worked really hard to learn their lines and impress their teacher.

At the next rehearsal, Miss Mallow arrived with Madame Angelwing, Poppy's ballet teacher.

"Class, Madame Angelwing is joining us today to take us through the dance routines. Please say 'Good Afternoon' to her and then we can begin."

But when the rehearsal started, Miss Mallow's mood quickly turned sour. Mimosa kept forgetting her lines; Lola had failed to learn the Cook's dance routine; Abi hadn't memorized the song tunes; and Ollie and Freddie did nothing but giggle in their Ugly Sister scenes.

Miss Mallow was very upset when it turned out that hardly anyone had bothered to do any work on the show; the members of the orchestra hadn't even practised their instruments. It was now the third week of rehearsals and they were no better than they had been at the first one. Miss Mallow felt extremely let down. What made things even worse was that she had now been embarrassed in front of Madame Angelwing. The dance teacher had lots of experience of putting on shows and had incredibly high standards.

Miss Mallow was also exhausted from working on the musical score with Mr Melody, not to mention discussing the set, scenery and costumes with Saffron and Lavender. She knew that the children couldn't be expected to stay up late or do as much as her, but she did expect them to learn their parts between rehearsals. After all, she had used the play to make fun class and homework tasks so that they didn't have too much to do. But she was determined not to give up.

"OK then, we'll all learn a new dance routine for the ball scene," she suggested. "This is the most difficult of all the dances, but Madame Angelwing and I think it will be spectacular and certainly worth the effort. We want all of you to weave in and out of each other, dancing an elegant Viennese waltz. Follow Madame's instructions and concentrate hard, children. I know you can do it! Please don't let me down. Madame Angelwing, over to you!"

At first, everyone stood up straight and smart as Madame Angelwing explained what they should do. But before long, much to Miss

Mallow's horror, some of the children started to lark around during the dance routine, making fun of Madame and trying out their own steps and ideas instead of following her instructions. Madame Angelwing was shocked. Her girls at the Lavender Lake School of Dance always did as they were told. She had never come across such unruly children – her presence alone was sufficient to silence her ballet girls, and their fear of her disappointment was enough to make them work hard. She didn't know what to do.

Miss Mallow was hurt that her beloved class were not putting all their efforts into the show and were treating Madame so badly: she soon became very cross indeed.

"Right!" she shouted. "I have tried everything to make this work. But clearly it hasn't been enough, so that's it, the show is off! There will be no show. You are not taking it seriously so you do not deserve to be given this opportunity."

"Aw, Miss Mallow!" protested one child.

"Be quiet, please. I've had enough of listening

to other people. I've done my best, but you haven't, and I'm sorry that it has come to this," said Miss Mallow as she began to gather up her things. "I will look forward to seeing you on Monday and I will be glad to return to how we were before the show. And as you leave, please apologize to Madame Angelwing for your extremely rude behaviour."

The children were in complete shock. They muttered their apologies to Madame Angelwing and went to meet their parents at the school gate. Here they found Miss Mallow telling all the mums and dads what had happened and why.

Their parents were disappointed, and some were rather cross, especially those who had put many precious hours into helping with the show and raising money for the hall. But they respected Miss Mallow and knew she would not have taken such a big decision lightly. They all recognized how important the show was to her and how much time she had dedicated to it.

Chapter Seven

All weekend Poppy and her friends wondered what would happen now. One minute they were cross with Miss Mallow for cancelling the show, the next they felt bad because they knew they could have put in more work themselves; but most of all they were angry with the people who had ruined everything by larking around in the rehearsal. Poppy and her friends would never have dared to behave like that in front of Madame Angelwing. It seemed there was nothing to do – nothing to talk about and nothing to look forward to – without the show.

Meanwhile Miss Mallow phoned Saffron.

"Oh, poor you!" said Saffron in disbelief. "I knew you were a bit low last week after the rehearsal, but are you quite sure this is what you want? It does seem a little drastic."

"I know, but I was so humiliated, and in front of Madame Angelwing as well. I thought my class respected me, but obviously not. I didn't realize quite what was involved in a show like this – I think it's just too much for me," sighed Miss Mallow.

"Of course it's not. How can I help? Let me think. Maybe if you had the rehearsal on a different day of the week, that might work better?" suggested Saffron softly. "I know I'm always shattered at the end of the week and I'm sure your

class is. I expect they are just finding it hard to concentrate. And you are tired out too."

"Yes, I'm shattered," agreed Miss Mallow. "It's so nice to have you to talk to, Saffron. I'll think it over. Perhaps you're right. Maybe I've been too rash – if we rehearsed at another time when they are fresher, that might just help."

"Yes, I really think it would, but for now you should just rest. Promise you'll take it easy over the weekend. Then see how you feel on Monday," said Saffron.

"OK, Saffron. And thanks!"

"Hey, that's what I'm here for. Call me any time."

At school on Monday Miss Mallow felt very much more energetic after a good rest. Although she was still upset and cross about the children's behaviour, she was sorry that she had called off the show and thought she had maybe been a bit harsh. Deep down she wanted to continue with it, but she didn't know if the children would want to now. She decided to see how they behaved that morning before she mentioned anything about the show.

Meanwhile, the children were all very sorry for upsetting their teacher and sad that the show they had all been so looking forward to had been cancelled. They were desperate for Miss Mallow to change her mind, but they decided not to say a word about the show until they had worked out whether she was still cross with them. So the teacher and her pupils spent the whole morning acting as if the show had never even existed!

At break, Poppy got the whole class together and told them that she had a plan.

"If we show Miss Mallow that we can work really hard when we try, then maybe she will un-cancel the show!" she began. "So why don't we practise the song from the first scene at lunch break and surprise Miss Mallow with it this afternoon!"

Everyone agreed that it was a great idea; this time they didn't even need a vote to come to a decision.

"The only thing is," said Honey, "I don't think Miss Mallow wants to do the show any more."

"Yeah, but if we sing the song really well and show her that we want to do the show more than anything, maybe she will change her mind. We've got to try," replied Poppy. "Let's meet in the music room after lunch! We'll practise it there. Abi can play the tune on the piano."

All through the morning lessons and lunch break, Miss Mallow was unable to concentrate on anything. She simply couldn't stop wondering what to do about the show. The children hadn't said a word about it, but she knew them well enough to know it was on their minds.

Maybe I should do something special to show them that I'm sorry for cancelling it, but that I expect them to work hard if they do want it to go ahead, thought Miss Mallow.

She decided to set up a recording machine in the gym with the help of Nick, the janitor. In the first class after lunch she would ask the children to come to the gym and perform the song from the first scene; she would record it, then play it back to them. She would treat them like proper stars – they would see how good they sounded and whether there was room for improvement! That would help to build their confidence: maybe then they would start taking the show more seriously. After the recording, depending on their reaction, she would ask them if they would be willing to carry on with it.

During the practice organized by Poppy, everyone was keen to do their very best, even those who had messed around and ruined the last rehearsal. Abi sat at the piano and played the "Poor Cinders" tune perfectly. Poppy arranged everyone in their correct positions.

"Oh, I do hope this persuades Miss Mallow to carry on," said Honey. "It's such fun when we all work together."

Sweetpea agreed. "I just wish I had worked harder before. Every time I tried to rehearse I just kept thinking of the night of the show and sort of daydreaming about it. Now I can see how much hard work we need to do."

"Come on, you lot," said Charlie. "Are we

doing this song or what?"

This time everyone concentrated hard, and after a few false starts they sang it beautifully.

"We sound brilliant!" Poppy grinned.

When the bell announcing the start of afternoon classes rang, she felt very nervous. "I just hope this works. I couldn't bear it if the show was off for ever," she said.

"Oh, Poppy," said Mimosa, "I'm sure Miss Mallow will be really proud of us – she'll have to let the show go on."

Once they were back in class, Poppy kept her fingers crossed behind her back and put up her other hand.

"Yes, Poppy?" said Miss Mallow.

"We have a surprise for you!"

"Ooh, how nice," said Miss Mallow. "I love surprises. The funny thing is, I have a surprise for you all too! It's in the gym. Why don't you tell me about your surprise first."

"Oh, well, we can do our surprise in the gym too!" said Mimosa.

"All right then, that sounds like a good idea," said Miss Mallow, wondering what the children could possibly have planned and feeling a little nervous about her surprise for them.

The class were wondering about Miss Mallow's surprise too. They were all very excited as they raced down to the gym.

"Shall we tell you our surprise first?" asked Poppy.

"Yes, go on then!" smiled Miss Mallow.

"Well, it's best that we show it actually. We've rehearsed the 'Poor Cinders' song and we are word perfect – to show you that we can do it when we try!" Poppy explained.

"I don't believe it!" said Miss Mallow. "My surprise for you is to record you singing that song to show you that you can do it!"

The children laughed.

"So the two surprises are sort of part of one big surprise!" observed Charlie.

"Yes – great minds think alike!" said Miss Mallow.

The children took their places, Miss Mallow pressed RECORD on her machine, Abi sat down at the piano and started playing the introduction, then the whole class sang "Poor Cinders"!

"Poor, poor Cinders, she's so very down,
Those Ugly, Ugly Sisters really make her frown.

Sweeping up their messes,
Washing all their dresses,

Cooking all their food,
While they are just so rude,

Brushing out their hair,
Folding underwear.

Poor, poor Cinders, she really needs a rest,
When will her father see that she is quite the best?"

Miss Mallow was entranced. The class had put heart and soul into their performance. As they took their bows, she smiled and clapped. She was very impressed – and surprised!

"Thank you, class, for making my day. That was lovely! I am so proud of you – see what a bit of practice can do!"

"It's so much nicer when she's not cross with us," whispered Ollie.

When they got back to their classroom, Miss Mallow played them the recording. Each and every one of them made a vow to practise as much as they could – if Miss Mallow agreed to go on with the show!

"Thank you for preparing that lovely song," said the teacher. "I'm sorry for getting so angry on Friday. I'm afraid I could see no way forward for the show. However, I've thought about it all weekend – and after your lovely performance today I've decided that, if you like, we will try again!"

The whole class cheered.

"This time, I think we should meet to rehearse every Saturday morning," said Miss Mallow. "That way you will be bright and fresh and ready to learn new things. How does that sound?"

"Great!" chimed the children.

"We're very sorry about our behaviour too, Miss Mallow," said Freddie.

All the children started to say their own apologies.

"Yeah, sorry, miss!" said Tom.

"We should have tried harder – sorry," said Sweetpea.

"Hurrah, the show's back on!" said Poppy.

Chapter Eight

The Saturday morning rehearsals were great fun and everyone worked hard over the next few weeks. Poppy and her friends wondered how they had ever existed without this in their lives.

One Saturday, when there was just under two weeks until the big day, and the tickets, posters and programmes were all printed, Nick, the janitor, told Miss Mallow that the builders had moved on to a new job.

"Does that mean the hall is finished?" she asked.

"Well, I suppose so. I've got the keys here

– let's go and have a look!" said Nick.

"Definitely!" said Miss Mallow. "We can work out where everything will go on the stage and check out the new lighting."

The children could hardly contain their excitement as their teacher led them towards the school hall.

"Ta-da!" said Miss Mallow as Nick opened the door and switched on the lights.

There was a gasp. The hall was covered in dust, bits of wood, tarpaulins, dust sheets and general builder's rubbish. It was a complete mess and looked far from finished. Miss Mallow was horrified.

"Quickly, children, everyone out! Let's go back to the gym," she instructed.

All my hard work will be for nothing if the hall isn't ready in time, she thought.

In the corridor on the way back to the gym they bumped into Mrs Milkthistle.

"Oh, Miss Mallow, I've been meaning to come and talk to you about the hall. I take it you've just come from there. I'm so sorry you had to find it in such a mess. You see, the thing is, the builders have finished the main work, but they've been called away on an emergency roof job at another school, so they haven't quite finished," explained the Headmistress.

"Oh!" said Miss Mallow. "When will they be back to finish it? The show is in less than two weeks."

"I'm afraid they're not going to be back for at least a month, so we'll have to make do," said Mrs Milkthistle. "Perhaps we could use the gym, or another venue like Cornsilk Castle or the Lavender Lake School of Dance?"

"But the whole point of the show is to celebrate the reopening of the school hall," said Miss Mallow. "We simply can't do it anywhere else and I don't have the time to clear up the mess myself. I just hope I have some good luck soon! The way things are, I'm not sure the show can go on."

When Poppy got home, she was very upset about the fact that the whole show might be cancelled – again. Mum was busy making lunch but when they sat down to eat, Poppy told her whole family all about the horrid mess.

"The hall looks so bad – even worse than it was before the builders came. I mean, there's no way we could do our show in there!" she said.

"Poor Holly!" exclaimed Mum. "She's going through the mill over this production, isn't she?

I wonder how we could help her, James. It would be such a shame to have to postpone the show after all the hard work that everyone has put in. I was looking forward to seeing it and I've even sorted out a babysitter for the twins!"

"Well, I suppose we could get a team together to clean it all up and take any rubbish they've left to the tip."

"Oh, that's a brilliant idea, James!" said Mum. "I'll help, and Granny Bumble will come too, I'm sure. Grandpa can babysit. Sally Meadowsweet will lend a hand – and Lily Ann

Peach and the Woodchesters, the Worthingtons, the Melodys – and the Turners too! I'm sure the whole village will join in. We owe it to Holly! She's worked so hard on this show, and so have all the children."

Mum started ringing around right away and before long everyone had agreed to meet at the school hall on Monday evening. They would bring cleaning things – dusters, brooms, vacuum cleaners, mops, buckets, cleaning fluids – along with rubbish sacks – and refreshments of course!

"We'll keep it a secret from Holly," said Mum at breakfast the next morning. "And Poppy, on Tuesday morning, perhaps you can somehow get her to go to the hall? That way she'll have a lovely surprise."

Poppy thought this was a great idea. "OK, Mum. I'll think of a plan!"

On Monday afternoon, Lavender Cotton got the key for the school hall from Nick, who knew about the secret clean-up and was coming

to help. Then, in the early evening, she and her cleaning team, numbering some twenty people, quietly let themselves in and put their plan into action.

"Gosh, Poppy wasn't kidding!" exclaimed Lavender when she saw the state of the place. "I can't believe the builders left it like this! Right, let's get started. Can I have a tidying group, a sweeping and hoovering group, plus a mopping group, please?

Sorry to sound a bit bossy, but I think we'll only get a result if we stick to a plan."

"This is just like being at home!" moaned Poppy's dad jokingly.

The hardworking teams did not finish until nearly midnight, and when they looked over their shoulders as they were leaving, they gasped in surprise. Suddenly they could see what a fabulous job the builders had done: it had definitely been worth all the effort. It was much better than they had hoped. The stage was newly edged with light beech wood. There were spotlights pointing down onto it, and wall lights all around the hall. Rows of smart new chairs in crimson red were revealed when they ripped off the polythene covers. The floor had been relaid with a lovely pale wood. The overall effect was stunning. The troop of workers had also hung some beautiful emerald-green velvet curtains, made by Saffron, on either side of the stage.

"What a great setting for the performance!" declared Mrs Woodchester.

Everyone agreed. They hoped their hard work would let Holly Mallow see that they were right behind her – and that she most definitely was not being left to do all the hard work on her own – like Cinderella!

Chapter Nine

On Tuesday morning Miss Mallow was looking very pale and tired. She was terribly worried about the hall. She had thought about putting off the show until a later date, but she didn't want to let the children down, especially now that they had put in so much effort. After she'd taken the register, she was muttering about the state of the hall and the fact that they'd not yet practised on the actual stage.

"Er, Miss Mallow, can we go down to the hall now, please?" asked Poppy. "We want to make some flower garlands for the ball scene and we need to see where we can hang them."

"Oh, Poppy, that is a good idea, but it's such a mess down there. I'm not sure we're even going to be able to use it," replied Miss Mallow.

"Oh, Miss Mallow, please can we go?" begged Poppy. "Maybe Cinderella and the Fairy Godmother have worked some magic on it!"

"If only real life were like that, Poppy," sighed her teacher. "Oh, all right, let's go and see where the garlands could go!"

She didn't want to sound too negative in front of the children, but flower garlands really were the last thing on her mind and she didn't even want to see the hall again. This whole production was designed to celebrate its reopening, but at the moment it looked as if an earthquake had hit it.

Poppy, Honey, Abi, Sweetpea and Mimosa led the way to the hall, pushed open the doors and switched on the lights . . .

Miss Mallow's face was a picture – first of confusion, then of delight.

"Please tell me I'm not dreaming this. It's so

EXIT
ABC

incredible. But how? When? I mean, who?" She was so thrilled with the transformation that she was in state of shock and was hardly making any sense.

"It was a working team of friends from the village who came in after school yesterday," explained Poppy, feeling very proud of her parents, who had organized the whole thing.

Miss Mallow was quite overwhelmed by the kindness of the local people. It brought a tear to her eye and it also meant that, after all the trials and tribulations, the show could go on after all.

The dress rehearsal the day before the show went well, even though everyone needed Saffron to adjust their outfits a little here and there and it took them a while to get used to using a different space. Miss Mallow was so proud of them. They were all very serious about their roles in the play and were now putting their hearts and souls into the production.

Before the final scene, the girls sat backstage in one dressing room, while the boys sat in another. Poppy loved having her make-up done by Lily Ann Peach from the Beehive Beauty Salon.

"Can I have a bit more sparkly eye shadow, please?" she asked. "The last scene is really sparkly."

"Oh, all right then," said Lily Ann. "But there'll be none left for the real show tomorrow if you girls keep putting it on double thick!"

Poppy and her friends were incredibly excited. They could hardly believe that the show had come round at last.

"We're really, definitely doing it now," said Mimosa. "I thought it would never happen."

Just then Miss Mallow called over her megaphone, "All children for the final scene come to the stage now."

The scene went like a dream. It was a highly emotional moment when the last word was spoken and the curtains were swished shut by Nick. Miss Mallow had never felt so proud.

"If you can do even half as well tomorrow night, I will be the happiest teacher in the world!" she declared.

The children went home with a bounce in their step and fell into their beds, completely exhausted.

Chapter Ten

On the night of the show, Poppy was more nervous than she had ever been in her life as she sat backstage. Her whole class were dying to catch a glimpse of Bryony Snow, who had been talked about so much.

The magazine editor arrived promptly and looked just as lovely as ever, wearing white flared trousers, a cropped lavender jacket with huge pearly buttons, and a large lime-green scarf. Her hair was lightly backcombed and tied in a ponytail. She wore lip gloss and soft peachy blusher. Bryony came backstage to say hello to the children and to wish Poppy luck, but there was no time to talk as Poppy had to get her make-up done and put on her costume.

Poppy looked stunning when she was ready. Even when Rose was in her non-ball outfit, she had a very pretty long red dress to wear. As for the ball gown, Poppy could hardly wait to appear in it. Maybe it was not quite as beautiful as Cinderella's, but it really suited her.

The gorgeous new green curtains swished open, revealing Act One, Scene One, which began in the kitchen with Cinderella and the Ugly Sisters. Soon it was Poppy's cue and Miss Mallow motioned from the wings that she should go on from the right.

Poppy's throat felt dry and tight. From somewhere deep inside her she felt the words come out: "Don't worry, Cinderella. You'll be the lucky one in the end. Just you wait. You're too kind and generous to suffer for long.

I'll look after you as much as I can!"

Cinderella smiled. "I wish I could believe you, Rose. I feel as if I'm going to grow old all alone, trapped in this house like a prisoner, with these wretched sisters and their mother. I never thought my father would allow it. He loves me, I know he does, but he's afraid of her, that's what it is. She has bullied him into treating me as their slave."

"You're the most hard-working person here and it seems you are the unluckiest, but that will change, I promise," said Poppy, as Rose.

Cinderella smiled again, then glanced at the sun dial. "Oh no! It's time for me do the Ugly Sisters' hair! I mustn't dawdle and chat when there's work to be done."

Rose shook her head and turned to look at the audience. "She is too good for them. I wish her luck could change!"

Then Poppy exited stage left and breathed properly for the first time in two days. She had done it. Somehow she had remembered her lines.

The whole class sang "Poor Cinders" next, which went smoothly and earned them huge applause from the audience. Poppy had no more lines until the ball scene, so she helped the other children get ready for their parts and enjoyed doing make-up for the Ugly Sisters – Freddie and Ollie! They looked very funny, wearing huge tent dresses with great big shoes and frizzy blond wigs. Mum had made them ugly bonnets, covered with fearsome bugs and beasties. Their make-up was vile as well – heavy and lumpy, with lipstick smeared messily round their mouths.

Honey was very sweet as the Fairy Godmother. She wore a frothy gold dress which shone in the stage lights, along with a lovely sparkly tiara which Poppy's mum had found in a charity shop in the City. Abi acted out her surprise at becoming a princess beautifully, making the audience feel happy for Cinderella. Everyone laughed when the pumpkin accidentally rolled down off the stage as it turned into a cardboard coach. But Poppy's very favourite bit was the ball scene. Even though everyone knew the story of the clock striking midnight, and the magic stopping, it was still incredibly exciting. The dresses were wonderful and the dancing was very elegant.

The wedding scene was quite beautiful, with all the children waltzing perfectly, just as Madame Angelwing had instructed them. Cinderella's wedding dress was based on the

one in Poppy's fairytale book. Even though Poppy was a little jealous, she thought Abi looked wonderful.

"If I ever get married, I will wear a dress just like that one!" she said to herself.

They finished the performance with "Wedding Bells", another of Miss Mallow's special songs.

"Ding-dong! Ding-dong!
Come and hear our wedding song!

The Prince has found a wife
With whom to live his life.

Cinders is so happy now,
Taking a wedding vow.

She can leave her work behind
And all of those who were unkind.

Ding-dong! Ding-dong!
Come and hear our wedding song!

Her sisters say 'Boo-hoo-hoo!
Whatever are we going to do?

There's dirty washing in a pile
And a list of jobs that lasts a mile.'

Cinders says: 'It's just too bad!
Now it's your turn to be sad!'

Ding-dong! Ding-dong!
Come and hear our wedding song!"

The children had to take several bows – the audience wouldn't stop clapping. And they sang the final song about four times after calls of "Encore!" from the audience!

The show, with its mixture of laughs and tears, gorgeous costumes and fabulous scenery, was a huge hit. When Poppy looked out into the audience during the final song, she could see Bryony in the front row beside Mrs Milkthistle. They were both enjoying themselves, laughing and clapping the whole time.

Poppy knew that all her special people were in the audience too – it meant so much to her to have Grandpa, Daisy, Edward, Mum, Dad

and all the other family members too. The twins hadn't come as they would have squirmed and made a noise, so they were being babysat by Uncle Daniel, who said Cinderella was a story he knew so well, he wouldn't mind missing the show on this occasion. Dad was filming the whole thing so they could all watch it whenever they wanted to.

When the clapping finally stopped and the children could sing no more, Miss Mallow came on stage and Poppy presented her with a bouquet of flowers provided by Sally Meadowsweet. Then Miss Mallow cleared her throat and started to speak.

"I am so proud to stand here tonight as the teacher of this brilliant class. We have had some hard times with this production, but it has all been worth it. Sometimes the high points of our children's young lives come when difficult struggles work out in the end. I cannot mention anyone by name as every single child has mattered equally in this production. So thank you, children, for being so amazing. I am proud of you all! And many, many thanks to all the grown-up helpers who have been unbelievably kind to me. As you all know, we are here tonight to celebrate the reopening of this fine hall, and I'm sure you will all agree that it is looking lovely – and the roof no longer leaks!"

There were cheers of agreement from the audience.

"So many people have helped to make this transformation possible, so let's just say what a great Team Honeypot effort it has been," she concluded. "And now, let's hear it for our special guest, Bryony Snow, editor of Buttons and Bows magazine."

Bryony Snow made her way onto the stage, with the audience clapping and cheering.

"It is an honour to be here and I have had a wonderful evening so far," she said. "I am so impressed by the show. I've laughed more than I've done in a long while, and also shed a couple of tears for poor Cinderella, beautifully played by Abigail Melody. I can't mention everyone by name, but you were all absolutely fabulous!

Thank you again for asking me to come. I will most certainly be writing a piece on your production for the next edition of Buttons and Bows – with photos!"

"Hurrah!" cried all the children, and Miss Mallow too.

"Now, I believe it's time for the after-show party!" announced Bryony. "Everyone over to the Hedgerows Hotel!"

At the party Miss Mallow came over to Poppy. "Thank you for the bouquet, Poppy, and for all your help over the last weeks," she said, hugging her pupil. "I want you to know that even though you weren't Cinderella, you have been the true Fairytale Princess throughout this production. You really are the star in my eyes."

Poppy smiled. "Thank you, Miss Mallow!" she said.

Buttons
& Bows!
Featuring the
Fantastic show
by
Rosehip
School
Cinderella!

Turn over to read an extract from
the next Princess Poppy book,
Pony Club Princess . . .

Chapter 1

Poppy ambled cheerfully down to Riverside Stables on Barley Farm. She couldn't wait to start riding over jumps on her chestnut pony, Twinkletoes. As she walked into the stable yard, she spotted her cousin Daisy tacking up her pony, Parsley, ready for a canter around the paddock.

"Hi, Poppy," called Daisy.

"Hi," replied Poppy, waving at her cousin.

"Did you get your Pony Club letter about taking part in the competition?" asked Daisy.

"Um, no, not yet. Did you get one?"

"Yes, it's just an 'acceptance to compete' letter,

which also explains what will happen at the competition. Look, I've brought it with me," said Daisy.

Poppy peered at the letter Daisy was holding.

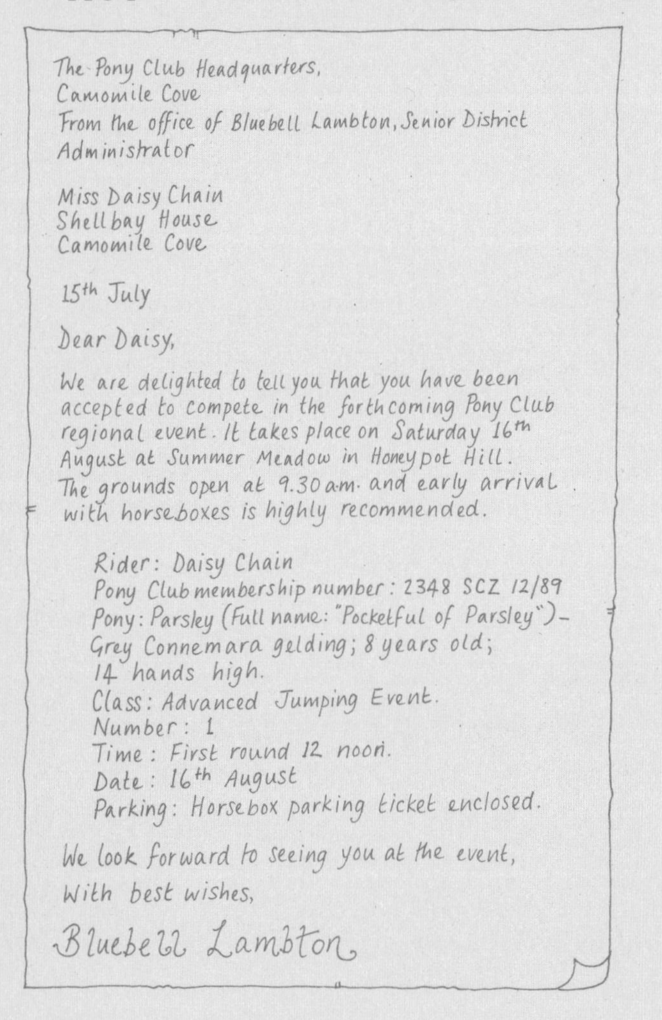

The Pony Club Headquarters,
Camomile Cove
From the office of Bluebell Lambton, Senior District Administrator

Miss Daisy Chain
Shellbay House
Camomile Cove

15th July

Dear Daisy,

We are delighted to tell you that you have been accepted to compete in the forthcoming Pony Club regional event. It takes place on Saturday 16th August at Summer Meadow in Honeypot Hill. The grounds open at 9.30 a.m. and early arrival with horseboxes is highly recommended.

Rider: Daisy Chain
Pony Club membership number: 2348 SCZ 12/89
Pony: Parsley (Full name: "Pocketful of Parsley") – Grey Connemara gelding; 8 years old; 14 hands high.
Class: Advanced Jumping Event.
Number: 1
Time: First round 12 noon.
Date: 16th August
Parking: Horsebox parking ticket enclosed.

We look forward to seeing you at the event,
With best wishes,

Bluebell Lambton

Poppy wished she had her letter too. It all sounded so grown up and exciting.

"Your letter will turn up soon," said Daisy kindly as she folded hers away.

"Yes, I expect so," replied Poppy. "The post hadn't even arrived when I left this morning, so it's probably at home right now. I've applied to join the Pony Club so that I can take part as a member."

"Cool, then we'll both be members," said Daisy with a smile. "Now, come on, we've got to do some practice!"

Down in the paddock, where they had a couple of old practice jumps set up, Daisy gave Poppy lots of tips about jumping.

"Shorten your reins and urge Twinkletoes forward with your legs, Poppy. That way you'll make sure he's under control and he'll be balanced for the jump. Then he'll soar over. It's a bit like flying!"

Poppy listened carefully to what her cousin said and was soon clearing the fences easily. Daisy was right – as they went over them, Poppy felt as though she and Twinkletoes were flying through the air.

"Wow!" said Daisy. "You're so good!

I'll have to make the fences a bit higher this time!"

Poppy beamed with pride and then tried the bigger jumps that Daisy had set up for her. She was concentrating so hard that she completely

forgot about her worries over the letter from the Pony Club.

Once she and Twinkletoes were completely exhausted, she watched admiringly as Daisy and Parsley jumped over really high fences. They were so good. Poppy was sure they would win their class in the competition.

When Daisy had finished, Poppy picked up two fallen apples for the ponies as a reward for a hard morning's work. Parsley ate his in a flash while Twinkletoes munched happily on his for ages. Then the two cousins led their ponies back to the stables, chatting about pony accessories.

"Shall we go to Ned's to get the ponies some treats for the competition?" suggested Daisy. "I might get Parsley a new numnah for under his saddle or some new ribbons for his plaits."

Poppy nodded enthusiastically. She loved Ned's, the saddler's shop in Camomile Cove. And it was great to hang out with Daisy as her best friend, Honey, had gone on her annual holiday with her mum and dad. This year they were in Los Angeles in America.

Poppy had missed out on taking part in the last Pony Club competition because she had been so busy preparing for her ballet exam, but she was determined that she would not miss out on this one. It was the local Pony Club's first ever competition to be held in Honeypot Hill. Poppy knew that all her family and friends would come down to watch and make a day of it. Her big ambition was to win

a red first-place rosette. She would fasten it proudly onto Twinkletoes' bridle and ride around the ring to a standing ovation from the crowd. She even saw herself riding at the next Olympic Games!

Poppy often got rather carried away when she was daydreaming. Thinking about it sensibly, she realized that, as it was going to be her first ever competition, she would be very lucky even to be placed in the top three. But more importantly, she needed the letter offering her a place, just like the one Daisy had been sent.

When they got back to Honeysuckle Cottage, Poppy ran through the house and burst into the kitchen.

"Mum! Mum! Has anything arrived in the post from the Pony Club?" she called, hoping that her letter had come.

"From the Pony Club?" asked Mum. "Um, no, there were just a few bills and a postcard from Honey. She says she's having a lovely time, but she misses you."

"Oh!" said Poppy, who would normally have been thrilled to receive a postcard from her best friend. "But Daisy has had a letter confirming her place in the Pony Club competition next month and her letter came this morning so mine should have come too."

Mum looked a bit flustered. She bit her lip anxiously.

"We filled in the application forms together," Poppy reminded her, beginning to feel rather worried, "and you said you'd post them off. Remember?"

"Um, to tell you the truth, darling, I don't remember actually posting those forms at all. Oh dear, I think it might have been on the day when the twins weren't very well a couple of weeks ago – I might have forgotten—"

"But, Mum!" exclaimed Poppy. "It's really important! It's my first ever Pony Club competition!"

"I'm sorry, darling. I just had a lot on my mind . . . Let me have a scout about my desk," said Mum. She soon reappeared with bright red cheeks, holding Poppy's application form, all correctly addressed and with a stamp in place, but just not posted.

"Poppy, I'm terribly sorry, I did forget. Don't worry, I'll take this over to the Pony Club offices and explain what's happened," said Mum. "Everything will be fine!"

"The only problem, Aunt Lavender," Daisy told her, "is that all applications were supposed to reach them by last Friday."